BAD KITTY DOES NOT LIKE EASTER

NICK BRUEL

ROARING BROOK PRESS • New York

Are you ready to find some
Easter eggs today, Kitty?

Kitty doesn't want to find SOME Easter eggs.
Kitty wants to find ALL the Easter eggs!

Kitty LOVES Easter eggs!
Easter eggs have CANDY!

The Easter Bunny hid **LOTS** of eggs, Kitty!

There are lots of **BLUE** eggs,
and lots of **RED** eggs,
and lots of **PURPLE** eggs!

But there is only one
GOLDEN EGG.
Whoever opens the GOLDEN EGG
will get the best thing EVER!

Better than **CANDY?!**
Kitty wants the best thing **EVER!**
Kitty wants the **GOLDEN EGG!**

Kitty wants the Golden Egg
more than anything.

Okay, kitties and Puppy—
On your mark . . .
Get set . . .
MEOW
MEOW
MEOW

GO!
Wow!
ZOOM

Look, Kitty!
BLUE eggs!

Kitty doesn't want blue eggs.
Kitty wants the GOLDEN EGG.

Look, Kitty!
RED eggs!

Kitty doesn't want red eggs.
Kitty wants the GOLDEN EGG.

Look, Kitty!
PURPLE eggs!

Kitty doesn't want purple eggs.
Kitty wants the
GOLDEN EGG.
MEOW
MEOW
MEOW

Kitty sees something!
It's round. It's golden.
Could that be the
GOLDEN EGG?!

Sorry, Kitty.
That's not the Golden Egg.

That's Puppy!

But he has

THE GOLDEN EGG!

Uh-oh!

Kitty doesn't have the Golden Egg.
She doesn't have **ANY** eggs.
No blue eggs. No red eggs. No purple eggs.

Kitty has no eggs at all.

Kitty doesn't like Easter eggs.
Kitty doesn't like Easter egg hunts.
Kitty doesn't even like the Easter Bunny.

KITTY DOES NOT LIKE EASTER!

Poor Kitty.

She won't get any candy.

WOW! Instead of candy, the Easter Bunny filled the eggs with fun challenges.

Big Kitty is writing a story about Chatty Kitty!
Chatty Kitty is singing a song about Stinky Kitty!
Stinky Kitty is writing a poem about Puppy!
Puppy is giving someone a present!

But Kitty isn't having any fun at all.

Look, Kitty!

Someone put something special in **YOUR** basket!

Go on, Kitty!

You know you
want to open it.

Open it!

HAPPY EASTER, KITTY

Chatty Kitty

Big Kitty

Stinky Kitty

That letter isn't from the Easter Bunny, Kitty.
That letter is from your friends.

Kitty thinks this is the best thing EVER!
PURRRRR

Kitty thinks she has the best friends EVER!
MEOW MEOW

Kitty likes Easter after all.
by Kitty
Draw a picture of you and your friends.

The Easter Bunny doesn't always leave candy inside those eggs.
Sometimes the Easter Bunny leaves little challenges. Try these, or make your own!

Feel free to photocopy this page and cut out the challenges so you don't damage your book. And you can always write your own challenges!

Draw a picture of you and your friends.

Give your friend a compliment.

Write a story about your friend.

Tell your friend a joke.

Sing a song about your friend.

Read a story to your friend.

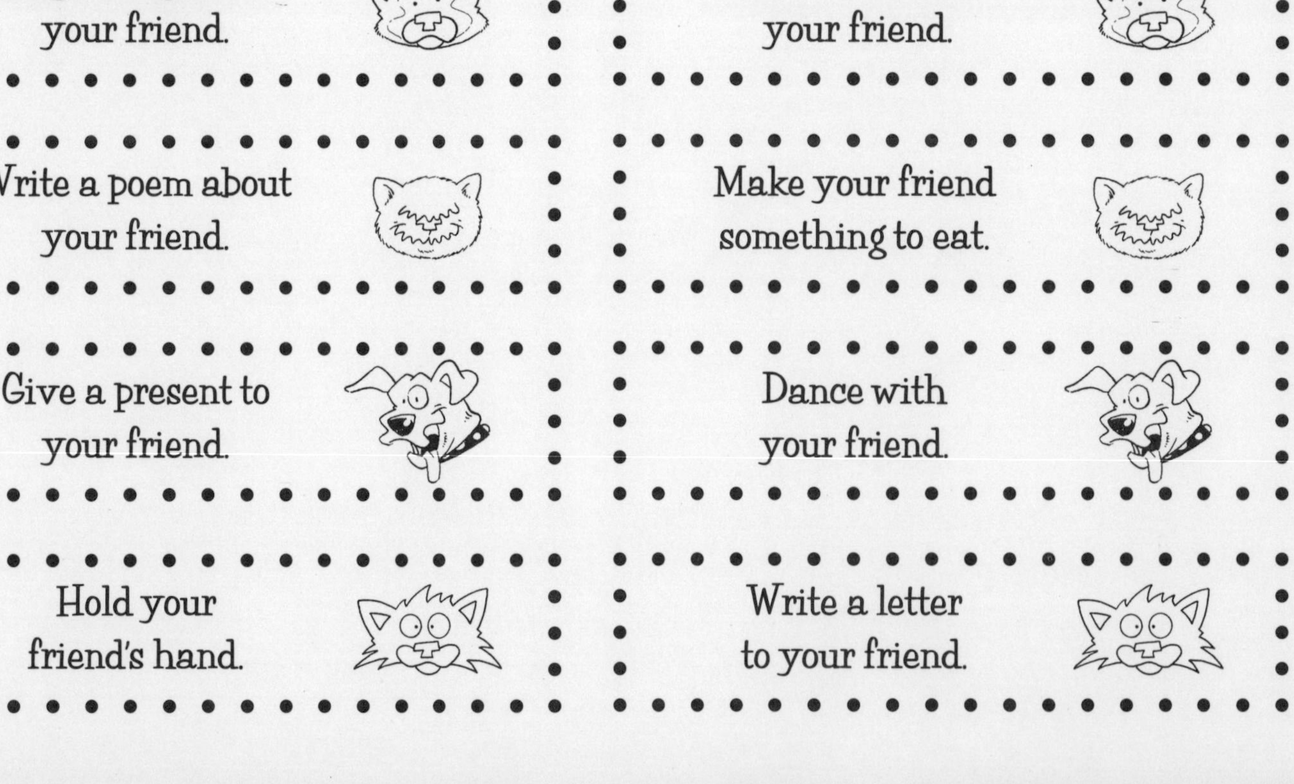

Write a poem about your friend.

Make your friend something to eat.

Give a present to your friend.

Dance with your friend.

Hold your friend's hand.

Write a letter to your friend.